Blow Away Soon

by **Betsy James**

illustrated by **Anna Vojtech**

G. P. Putnam's Sons   New York

G. P. Putnam's Sons, a division of The Putnam & Grosset Group,

200 Madison Avenue, New York, NY 10016.

G. P. Putnam's Sons, Reg. U.S. Pat. & Tm. Off.

Published simultaneously in Canada.

Printed in Hong Kong by South China Printing Co. (1988) Ltd.

Designed by Donna Mark. Lettering by Colleen.

Text set in Cochin.

Library of Congress Cataloging-in-Publication Data

James, Betsy. Blow away soon / by Betsy James; illustrated by Anna Vojtech. p. cm.
Summary: While building a blow-away-soon for the wind, a little
girl learns from her grandmother that some things are to let go of
and some are to keep for a good long time.
[1. Winds—Fiction. 2. Loss (Psychology)—Fiction.] I. Vojtech, Anna, ill.
II. Title. PZ7.J15357B1 1995 [E]—dc20 93-27135 CIP AC

ISBN 0-399-22648-6

1 3 5 7 9 10 8 6 4 2

First Impression

For Jim, who taught me how to build them
—B. J.

For Judy Sue
—A. V.

I live with my grandma in the very last house. The wind blows at night.

"Nana!" I call.

Nana comes. "How's my Sophie?"

I tell her, "I don't like the wind."

"That old wind," says Nana. "Listen to her blow!"

"She blew away my cowboy hat," I say. "She blew my Christmas jacket off the line and rolled my wagon out into the street."

"Don't you mind her," Nana says. "She's just doing her work. That wind's a tough old lady, just like me."

"You're not old!" I say. "You won't leave me ever, will you, Nana?"

"I'm not leaving anybody for a good long time," says Nana. "Now snuggle down, get cozy, and come morning you can build that old lady wind a blow-away-soon."

"What's a blow-away-soon?"

"Your grandpa taught me," Nana says. "Come morning, I'll show you."

But when morning comes there is no wind.

"She's resting someplace," Nana says. "An old lady likes to rest from time to time. Shall we go find her?"

We scramble down the sandy red track. In front of us the yellow grass begins to yank and nod.

"Here comes that wind," says Nana. "When she blows, the grass bends and shakes off its seeds. That's how next year's grass gets planted."

I pick a stem of grass and carry it like a flag. "When do we build a blow-away-soon?"

"Bring your flag to the top of the hill," says Nana, "and you'll see."

The wind sighs. Sand stings me, and I squint my eyes.

"Watch that old wind sweep," says Nana. "Good as if she had a broom."

Our shoes leave footprints. My feet get silly, sliding around. I say, "My shoes are full of sand."

"That's the best way to carry it," Nana says. "Sand comes in handy for a blow-away-soon."

The wind gets pushy. Birds are tipping around in the sky.

"Those birds think the wind is fine," says Nana. "What would a bird do without wind to slide on?"

I find a blue feather. "For you!" I call.

Nana puts it in her buttonhole.

Now we're climbing up among the rocks. They make cliffs, canyons, towers, walls.

Nana puffs and pants. We're almost to the top. But I call, "Wait, Nana!"

"Good," she laughs. "An old lady likes to rest from time to time."

"Look, I found a shell." But shells are in the sea. Not in stony hills.

"Here where we're standing there was an ocean once," says Nana. "There were rainstorms and huge waves. The wind blew even then.

"That ocean dried up to stone. The wind's been carving it ever since. Listen!"

The wind hisses like waves.

"That's how she sounds when she's carving rock," says Nana. "She carved out that shell for you, from the shore of an old sea."

"Can I keep it?"

"For as long as you like," says Nana.

We climb and climb, until the sky is wide all over. There's nothing here—just air, and that's what wind is made of.
Nana says, "Sophie, can you find a good big stone?"
"Here's one."

"Perfect. Now put another stone on top of it. Then another, and another. Build it tall."

"Is that all?" I ask. "That's a blow-away-soon? That's easy."

"The hard part's this," says Nana. "You ask yourself: What shall I give the wind for her to blow away?"

I think about it. "I could give her my grass flag. She makes the grass shake down its seeds."

"Good idea," Nana says. "Now your grass belongs to the wind. What else shall we give her?"

"Sand!" I take my shoes off. "It's full of our footprints." I sprinkle it on top. "What else?"

Nana pulls the feather from her buttonhole and winks at me. I smile and tuck the feather between two stones.

"Is that everything?" asks Nana.

I put my hand in my pocket. I uncurl my fingers. The shell is cool and small.

"I could give her this," I say.

But I don't want to. It's *my* shell. It's all that's left of an old sea.

The wind blows. Nana puts her arms around me.

"Sophie," she says, "some things blow away, but some things stay. Some things are to let go of, but others are to keep for a good long time."

I look down at the shell in my hand.

Nana asks, "Is there anything you'd like to keep even more than that shell?"

"You," I say. "I want you to live forever."

"I will live for a good long time," says Nana.

I put my shell on the blow-away-soon. "The wind can have that," I say.

Nana smiles. The wind lifts our hair.

"You, Wind," she says. "This is Sophie, my granddaughter. She loves you because you're an old lady, just like me. She's giving you some things to blow away soon, because she knows there are other things that she can keep for a good long time."

The wind says nothing. But the grass stem bends, shaking off seeds. The red sand sifts and hisses, blowing away. The blue feather twinkles through the air like a flying bird, and the shell rocks a little, as if it were alive.

"There's the old lady," I tell Nana, "doing her work."

We head back down the hill. I run, and Nana walks, and the wind follows us home.